For my brother Dan

10 9 8 7 6 5 4

Printed in China

Chronicle Books LLC
680 Second Street
San Francisco, CA 94107
www.chroniclebooks.com

Illustrations by Adam McCauley
Design by Alethea Morrison
Typeset in Triplex, Avenir, and Circus Mouse

ISBN 978-0-8118-3443-8

ACKNOWLEDGMENTS
To my extraordinary family: Mike Eldon, Evelyn
Mungai, Russell and Louise Knapp, Gaby
Eldon, Ruth Eldon, and Odette Bishop, who have
held my hand through this journey.

With special thanks to my mother Kathy Eldon for
her friendship and unconditional love, and thanks
to my star people.

With gratitude to Dr. Ernest Katz for his kind
contributions and with appreciation to Carey Jones
and Debra Lande.

*Visit www.creativevisions.org to find out more about
the work of Kathy and Amy Eldon.*

ANGEL CATCHER for Kids

A JOURNAL TO HELP YOU REMEMBER
THE PERSON YOU LOVE WHO DIED

by AMY ELDON

CHRONICLE BOOKS
SAN FRANCISCO

INTRODUCTION
for grownups

When someone dies, it's hard enough for adults to cope, but children often have an even tougher time dealing with the loss of a loved one. All too often, children's feelings are overlooked—with tragic consequences. Lacking the vocabulary to express their feelings, kids can act out, become depressed, confused, aggressive, and angry, or bottle up their feelings. Sometimes children appear to be fine because they have a hard time expressing how they feel in words.

Angel Catcher for Kids guides young readers through the five stages of grieving (shock and denial, anger, bargaining, depression, acceptance), offering simple prompts to help children express their feelings through words and drawings. The journal also gives the child's parent or caregiver an opportunity to explore the grieving child's thoughts and feelings in a safe and comforting way. It can also help adults find the words to express their own thoughts and feelings during a difficult time.

One of the hardest challenges for children facing loss is to hang on to memories of the person they love who has died. This journal will serve as a treasured keepsake and memory bank for the child to enjoy and reflect upon later in life.

Let the child fill in the journal at his own pace—choosing the pages that fit with what he is feeling on that particular day. It is okay for the child to put the book away for a while and return to it, when it feels comfortable. You might want to help create a special box of memories, which the child can fill with photos, mementos, and other treasures, which will remind him of the person who has died.

Use this journal with the child as a way to deepen communication, to cry, to laugh, and to remember your loved one. As hard as it is, grieving can be a gift, if we use it to examine our own lives and come closer to those we love.

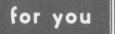

Death is nothing to be afraid of. In fact, everyone will die sometime. But it is really tough when someone you love dies. Right now is a confusing time; you can go from crying one minute to laughing out loud the next. It is important to just feel it all and *GET IT OUT!!* Don't bottle anything up because those yucky feelings will just come back and grab you when you aren't looking.

You probably have a lot of questions about death, so don't be afraid to ask someone to help you understand what's going on. You might get some different answers because people have many different ways of dealing with death. This journal is to help you make sense of it all. You can fill this book in when you feel happy, sad, mad, or confused. This is your book and there are no rules. Start anywhere and fill in the pages in any order. You can fill it in by yourself or share it with someone else. Some days you might feel brave, and other days you may feel scared and that's okay too.

Have fun with the drawing pages—scribble, paint, or paste. Use them so you can remember more about the person who you love, or just doodle if you feel like it. Sometimes, it's easier to draw feelings instead of trying to find words to describe them.

I wrote this book when my brother Dan died and I felt like my whole world was turned upside down. I was really sad. It was like I went on a long journey inside myself before I could feel happy again. I had to go through the sadness in order to come out the other end and smile again. I still miss my brother every day. I think of him when I see a flock of birds, and one of the birds leaves the flock and sails off into the sky. Even though I can't see the bird anymore, I know it's still flying. Now I just feel lucky that I had Dan in my life and that makes my happiness much bigger than my sadness.

I hope this book makes your journey a gentle one and your happiness grows and grows.

Love,

Amy

A Picture of You and Me

Blue Day

Today I feel sad. Here is how I look...

Weird

Everyone seems to be acting weird. I'm not sure what is going on. Here is what happened...

I feel...

To make myself feel better I will...

Fly

When you died, the real you left your body—I guess that is what some people call the soul of a person. I know the body you left behind isn't all of you.

This is what we are going to do with your body...

Here is where I think your soul is now...

Last Time I Saw You

Last time I saw you I wanted to say...

I wanted you to say...

I felt...

Now I feel...

Remembering

These are some of the last memories we shared...

One Last Thing

Before you died, I wish I had told you...

Before you died, I wish you had told me...

Saying Goodbye

The funeral is over. Here's what happened...

I felt...

The most important thing about it for me was...

Scary Day

Today I feel afraid. Here is what I am scared of...

Here is what I think you would tell me to do...

THINKING OF YOU HELPS ME TO FEEL BRAVE.

What Does It Mean to Die?

I am having a hard time figuring out what happens when someone dies.
Here's what I think it is all about...

Here's what I still don't understand...

Here is who I am going to ask about it...

Missing You

I miss you. I miss the way we used to...

I miss the way you...

I want to tell you about...

I LOVE YOU.

Blah Day

I don't feel like doing anything. I don't want to see anyone. I feel...

I wonder if I will ever be happy again. To cheer myself up I will...

Feel Like Crying

I feel like crying today. I think I feel like this because...

I know it's okay to cry and I know I will feel better if I do cry, or scream, or...(fill in whatever you feel like doing, and then go do it!)

HERE GOES!

Sad Today

Here's how I look outside...

Here's how I look inside...

Guilty

Sometimes I feel guilty. Here is what I feel guilty about...

I think this is what you would say to me...

Roller Coaster

Today I feel like I'm on a roller coaster ride. Sometimes my stomach hurts. To calm it down, I will...

Stay

Sometimes I get scared that someone else special might die too. I guess that just because one person dies it doesn't mean someone else has to die too.

I need to talk to someone about this. Here's who I will talk to...

Going Nuts

I am so mad! I want to scream. To get all these mad feelings out, I am going to...

Punch my pillows.

Hit things with a foam bat.

Stomp on bubble wrap.

Pound some clay with my fists.

Squeeze all my muscles and let go.

Yell and shout!

And then I will...

Mad Sad

I get mad when I think we will never be able to...

I feel sad when I know you won't see me...

Here is a drawing of me so you can see how I look today...

Acting Strange

It is hard for other kids to understand how I am feeling. They don't really know what happened. Here's what I can say to explain why I am acting strange...

Where Are You?

I wonder where you are now. I think you are...

Dreaming of You

I dreamed about you last night. This is what my dream was about...

Here is a picture of it...

Giggles

Something funny happened today. I want to tell you all about it! Here's what happened...

Happy Sad

Here's how you looked when you were happy...

Here's how you looked when you were sad...

Photo Album

My favorite pictures of you!

More Fun Pictures

My Favorite Photos

Somewhere Out There

I like to think that even though I can't see you, you are watching over me. Here's what I think you look like now...

Listening

When I close my eyes and sit still and listen, I can hear your voice inside me. Here's what you are saying...

Making You Proud

Today you would be proud of me. Here's what happened...

Here's what I think you would say to me...

Good Grief

I feel yucky again today. I guess they call that grieving; it is how you feel after someone has died. When you are grieving you can feel scared, sad, confused, mad, guilty, and sometimes even happy. I know it is important to feel my feelings because then I can get through them and feel better.

Here is how I feel right now...

To feel better I can: share my feelings with someone else, draw a picture, write about how I feel, or...

Here is who I am going to share my feelings with...

Tossing and Turning

When I can't sleep, I am thinking about...

I think you would say...

Next time I can't sleep I am going to...

Holding You

Today I need you with me. I am going to draw a picture of you and me together, and I am going to take the picture with me all day long.

--------------------------------CUT HERE--------------------------------

Helping Me Help

I know that you would tell me one way to feel better is to help someone else. Here's what I will do...

I Feel Alone

Sometimes I feel mad at you for leaving me. I know you didn't mean to go, but I feel alone. Now I am going to close my eyes and remember what it was like to be with you.

I remember how we used to...

Wishing

I wish...

I hope...

I need...

I want to try...

Best Day Ever

Today I am going to remember all the good things we used to do together.
Here's what happened on one of my favorite days with you...

Big Hug

Here's you holding me (draw or paste in a picture here)...

Happy Birthday to Me!

It's my birthday today. I am _____ years old.

Today I feel...

On my birthday we used to...

I am going to remember you by...

Happy Birthday

Today is your birthday. You would be _____ years old.

On your birthday we used to...

This is what I am going to do for you today

A Day to Remember

Today is a day to remember. You died on this day, _____ year (s) ago.

I am going to remember you by...

Holidays

Holidays just aren't the same without you. Today is...

Here's how I am feeling about today...

I remember how you used to...

To make myself feel better I am going to...

New Beginnings

Since you died, I feel different. Here are some good changes...

Here are some not so good changes...

Laughing Out Loud

I can't stop laughing when I remember...

You always laughed when...

I always laughed when you...

Right now I am going to close my eyes and picture you smiling. I want to laugh more often. Here is what I will do to make me smile...

Memories

I never want to forget the special times we shared together. Here are some of my favorite memories...

Never Forget

I never want to forget how you...

I always want to remember what happened when you...

Treasure Chest

I have a box that I am going to fill with my memories of you. I will put in pictures and stories, things that remind me of you, and things you gave me. Here's what I will put in my box...

Favorites

Your favorite song...

My favorite song...

Your favorite movie...

My favorite movie...

Your favorite game...

My favorite game...

More Favorites

Your favorite food...

My favorite food...

Your favorite clothes...

My favorite clothes...

Your favorite ice cream...

My favorite ice cream...

Your favorite people...

More Favorites

My favorite people...

Your favorite pet...

My favorite pet...

Your favorite place...

My favorite place...

Your favorite book...

My favorite book...

A Letter to You

I'm going to write you a letter and tell you some things I forgot to say.

Dear _____,

A Letter to Me

Here's what I think you would say to me.

Dear   ,

I Love You

I love you. I love you because...

Thank You

You will live in me always. Your words, your heart, your soul are all part of me. My heart is full of your memories. Thank you for the gift of your life. I will never forget you.

(space to write or dream)

HELPFUL READING

Boritzer, Etan. *What is Death?* Santa Monica, CA: Veronica Lane Books, 2000. Introduces children to the idea of death using examples of beliefs from various different religions.

Conley, Bruce H. *Butterflies, Grandpa, and Me.* Springfield, IL: Human Services Press, 1987. A gentle introduction to the concept of dying.

Dyregrov, Atle. *Grief in Children: A Handbook for Adults.* London: Jessica Kingsley Publishers, 1990. A handbook for teachers, social workers, counselors, parents, and others faced with the task of understanding children in grief and trying to help them.

Grollman, Earl. *Explaining Death to Children.* Boston: Beacon Press, 1965. A book that helps parents and teachers understand children, death, and how to communicate what is happening.

Rosen, Helen. *Unspoken Grief: Coping with Childhood Sibling Loss.* Lexington, MA: Lexington Books, 1986. An overview of children's comprehension of death, childhood bereavement, and parental loss.